OTHER BOOKS BY INEZ HOGAN

The Twin Series

Twin Colts
Monkey Twins
Twin Deer
Twin Seals
Mule Twins
Twin Lambs
Raccoon Twins

Kangaroo Twins
Twin Kids
Elephant Twins
Bear Twins
Giraffe Twins
Koala Bear Twins
Twin Kittens

The Nicodemus Books

Nicodemus and the Goose
Nicodemus and His Gran'pappy
Nicodemus and the Gang
Nicodemus and the Houn'dog
Nicodemus and the Little Black Pig

Nicodemus and the New Born Baby
Nicodemus and His New Shoes
Nicodemus Laughs
Nicodemus Runs Away
Nicodemus and Petunia

Nicodemus and His Little Sister

The Nappy Books

Nappy Chooses a Pet
Nappy Planted a Garden
Nappy Wanted a Dog
Nappy Is a Cowboy

The Read-To-Me Books

About Nono, the Baby Elephant
About the Littlest Cowboy
About Peter Platypus
About Charlie

Nappy Has a New Friend

Books Not In Series

We Are a Family
World Round
Runaway Toys
A Party for Poodles
A Bear Is a Bear
The Upside Down Book
Me
The Little Ones
The Big Ones

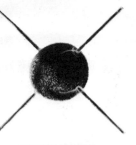

THE
LITTLEST
SATELLITE

story and pictures by

Inez Hogan

NEW YORK

E. P. DUTTON & CO., INC.

1958

Dedicated to

HENRY M. LEUCHTMAN

Photo by John B. Leuchtman

"What is the moon?" asked Quizzy.
"Tell me. What is the moon?"

He had to ask questions over and
over because no one listened to him.

Quizzy lived underground.

He was the littlest gnome and all
of the other gnomes called him Quizzy
because he was inquisitive—always
asking questions.

He wanted to find out about everything.

"What is the moon?" asked Quizzy.

The grown-up gnomes were busy
getting ready to go up on earth to
dance in the moonlight.

But Grampy, the oldest gnome,
stopped to answer little Quizzy.

"The moon is the moon," said Grampy.
"When you're bigger, you will go up on
earth and see the moon. Then you'll
know."

While Quizzy was growing up, he kept on asking questions.

And, at last, the time came when he was big enough to follow the other gnomes through the dark underground tunnels and out on earth.

Then he saw the moon. "Gee whizican! WHAT IS IT?" he shouted,

"Can't you see?" said Grampy. "It's the moon."

Quizzy didn't answer. He just stood there staring at the moon and thinking. Of course, I can see the moon. I know now what it *looks like*. I know it's round and bright and beautiful.

And I know *where* the moon is ... way up high in the sky.

But I still don't know *what* it is.

Quizzy kept on staring up and wondering.

Then, all of a sudden, a dark shadow passed over the moon.

"What's that?" shouted Quizzy. "WHAT'S THAT?"

The gnomes were too busy dancing in the moonlight to answer.

Quizzy asked too many questions anyway.

But a good little fairy who happened
to be flying by, heard Quizzy's question
and she stopped to answer:
　　"That's a witch.
　　She flies by night
　　High in the sky
　　In the pale moonlight.
　　Since time began
　　She has flown on her broom.
　　The witch will fly
　　Till the day of doom."
And the fairy disappeared.

Quizzy stared up into the sky
wondering about the wonderful witch
who could fly to the moon.

Then he saw her! The witch
on her broomstick, flying down, down,
down. And Quizzy ran, ran, ran to
where she landed on earth.

He was out of breath. "Oh, Mrs. Witch,"
he gasped. "You can fly to the moon on your
magic broom. I saw you. Please, please, tell me.
What is the moon?"

"Catch your breath, little one," said
the witch. "The moon, of course, is the moon."

"Of course," cried Quizzy, "that is
what we call it. But what *is* it?
I'm called Quizzy and I *know* what I am.
I'm a gnome. But what is the moon?"

"I'll ask him," said the witch.
"Fiddle dee dee,
And lack-a-day
Up to the moon, broom,
Whisk awa-a-y."

When the witch came back to earth, it was almost daylight. "I must be off to my cave. I'm sleepy," she said.

"What is the moon?" cried Quizzy. "Did he tell you?"

"The moon told me," said the witch, "that he is a satellite. That's all he said, except he has to keep going in his orbit. So, now, inquisitive little imp, you don't know any more than you did before."

And off went the old witch to her cave, mumbling, "Moon . . . satellite . . . orbit. Hee, hee, hee, and fiddle, dee, dee."

Quizzy sat on a rock, looking up.
Now I know that the moon is a satellite,
he thought. "But WHAT IS A SATELLITE?"
he shouted.

Then he heard a tiny, tinkly tune
and the good fairy appeared. "Why don't you
ask the moon?" she said. "The moon *is*
a satellite, so *he* would know what a
satellite is."

"Of course," said Quizzy, "but how
will I get up there?"

"The witch flies up every night,
Be kind to her, perhaps she might
Let you ride on her broomstick."

"Of course," said Quizzy, and he ran to the witch's cave. The witch was sound asleep.

I'll clean up her cave, thought Quizzy. That will be a good deed.

So he swept and dusted and polished the witch's cauldron.

And when she woke up, the witch said,

"Whippity, Whoppity! What do I see?
A gnome has cleaned my cave for me.
Now, little Quizzy, what can I do—
What can I do for you?"

"Fly me to the moon," said Quizzy.

"Hop on my broomstick," said the witch.

"Here I am," shouted Quizzy, "face
to face with the moon. It's magic."

"Of course," said the witch, "my broom
is magic. Now, speak up. You're always
asking questions. Speak up."

"Uh-uh, Mr. Moon," stammered Quizzy.
"What—what is the moon?"

"Ho! Ho!" said the moon. "I'm a
satellite."

"Of course," said Quizzy, "but what *is* a satellite?"

"A satellite is a follower," said the moon. "I'm an earth satellite, so I follow the earth around."

"Around what?" asked Quizzy.

"Just around," said the moon. "But I have to stay in my orbit, or I'd bump right into the earth."

"What's an orbit?" asked Quizzy.

"An orbit is a path," said the moon. "My orbit runs around and around the earth."

"I can run around and around a tree," said Quizzy.

"That's easy," said the moon. "The tree is standing still."

"Isn't the earth standing still?"

"Heavens, no!" said the moon. "The earth moves in its orbit, too."

Quizzy looked down. "Gee!" he said. "The earth doesn't look as if it's moving. Oh, my cap! My cap!"

"Look!" shouted Quizzy. "My cap fell off. It's just floating around in space. It didn't fall down. Why?"

Quizzy reached for his cap and he fell off the broom and he floated about in space, too.

"You'll have to rescue him, witch," said the moon. "My gravity is not strong enough to pull him back."

"Fiddlesticks!" said the witch, as she caught Quizzy by the seat of his pants. "Gravity, gravity, what on earth is gravity?"

"Gravity," said the moon, "is what holds you on earth. If you didn't have a magic broom, you couldn't fly up here.

"Men on earth have been trying to get up here for years. And they'll do it, too. They don't have a magic broom, but they have scientists who are building rockets to shoot up here."

"What are scientists?" asked Quizzy. "And what are rockets?"

"Scientists are smart men. They're inquisitive like you, Quizzy. They want to find out all about me and about space, so they ask questions.

"They can't get up here because gravity pulls them back to earth. And they don't know about magic.

"But they know about science and that's almost like magic. They'll get up here soon because they're building a satellite right now. And they're going to shoot it up here with a rocket.

"The satellite will stay up here, too. It will have an orbit and will travel around the earth and send messages back to earth."

"How?" asked Quizzy. "How can a satellite send messages?"

"They'll put instruments inside their little satellite," said the moon. "Instruments that will send messages back to earth from outer space."

"What are instruments?" asked Quizzy.
"And what is outer space?"

"One question at a time," said the moon.
"Have you ever heard of a radio?"

"Yes," said Quizzy. "A radio talks to
you."

"Well, a radio is an instrument
that sends messages. And outer space
is where you are now ... and you'd
better get back to earth. Good-by."

On the way back to earth Quizzy
didn't ask any questions. He had too
much to think about,—satellites—orbits—
gravity—scientists—rockets—instruments and
outer space.

It was daylight when they landed
on earth. The witch rushed to her cave
to sleep. And Quizzy said, "Thank you,"
and went to sleep in his underground
cave.

He dreamed that the gnomes deep
in the earth were building a tiny
satellite. The littlest satellite.

Quizzy was awake before midnight.
He woke up his friends Teckny and Tinker.

"What's the matter?" they asked.

"Sh-sh—" whispered Quizzy.
"I had a dream. We gnomes built a
satellite, the littlest satellite. It was
that way in the dream. Tiny."

"What are you talking about?" asked
Teckny.

"It's top secret," whispered Quizzy.
"Come on outside."

Teckny and Tinker followed Quizzy out. The moon was high in the sky. The fairies, sprites, elves, and gnomes were dancing in the moonlight.

"We have no time for dancing," said Quizzy. "What I'm going to tell you is top secret. Listen. I've been up to the moon. The witch took me up on her broomstick. She's been flying up there for thousands of years, but she never found out anything. She's not inquisitive. But I asked questions. I found out plenty."

"What?" asked Teckny and Tinker.

"The moon told me that men on earth are building a little satellite to send up in space. Now we're going to build the littlest satellite. Right here in our underground workshops.

"I know something about satellites and rockets, but we'll have to find out more."

"How?" asked Teckny and Tinker, both at one time.

"Well," said Quizzy, "when people want to find out about anything, they go to a library.

"Libraries are full of books about everything. We can look at books about satellites. Some books even have pictures. We can see what rockets and satellites look like.

"Let's go," said Quizzy. "We'll get there before the library opens."

So, just as the moon was setting, the three little gnomes turned their magic caps three times and sang:

"Magic cap turn one—two—three.
Send me where I want to be."

And that's how Quizzy, Teckny,
and Tinker arrived at a library.

"What a wonderful place!" said Teckny.

"Let's get to work," said Quizzy.

He found a book about scientists and what they thought about satellites.

Teckny looked into technical books and saw plans for rockets and satellites.

Tinker climbed around in the stacks of books on shelves and pulled down books that showed how satellites and rockets were built.

When the library opened and people came, the three little gnomes turned their caps three times and wished themselves back to their homes underground.

And with their heads full of knowledge, the three little gnomes went to sleep.

When they woke up, it was
night and all the other gnomes were
going outside to dance in the moonlight.

Quizzy ran after them, shouting,
"Stop—Stop—No dancing tonight."

The gnomes stood still and looked
surprised.

"Listen!" shouted Quizzy.
"We gnomes are going to build
a satellite ... a tiny moon, to send
up into space."

"What's he talking about?" mumbled
the gnomes.

"You'll find out," cried Quizzy.
"It will be fun. All gnomes like
to work and this will be nice, hard work.

"Teckny and Tinker and I
have found out how to make
a satellite. But we'll need all of you
to help. We'll work day and night.

"We'll build our own satellite—
The littlest satellite."

"Hurrah!" shouted the gnomes.
"Let's get to work."

And then, for a time, there was no dancing in the moonlight.

The gnomes were busy in their underground workshops. Deep in the earth they worked with magic skill building the littlest satellite.

Day and night they hammered and banged and bent and molded to build a rocket, big enough to carry the tiny satellite up into space.

The moon knew what was going on. But the fairies, elves, and sprites wondered why the gnomes didn't come out to dance in the moonlight.

They didn't find out because Grampy stood guard at the entrance to the caves.

Night after night the gnomes worked, checking every wire, bolt, nut, and screw. Until at last, it was ready to launch.

They carried the big rocket out of the cave.
Quizzy held on to the nose of the
rocket because that's where the tiny
satellite was hidden.

The gnomes were excited but
very quiet.

The fairies, sprites, and elves came out
from behind rocks, staring in wonder
at the big, shiny rocket.

At last the rocket was set
up ready to launch. Ready to
carry the littlest satellite into space.

"Firing time!" shouted Quizzy.
"Count down! Four—three—two—one—
FIRE!"

There was a burst of scalding steam.
The air shook with thunder.

But the rocket didn't budge
from the earth.

The gnomes groaned "Oh-o-o-o."

"Something has been forgotten,"
shouted Quizzy. "It can be fixed."

Teckny and Tinker were already
at work. It was just one small
piece of wire.

Nothing wrong that couldn't be
fixed.

And again the big, shiny rocket
was ready to launch.

The gnomes were very quiet.
The elves, sprites, and fairies
held their breath.

"Count down!" shouted Quizzy.
"Four—three—two—one—
FIRE!"

With a roar like thunder, up
zoomed the rocket. Up—up—up!
The littlest satellite was on its
way into space!

The gnomes shouted.

The fairies danced.

The moon grinned.

The Littlest Satellite was in space, rushing breathlessly around in its orbit.

Beep! Beep! Beep!